GOLD
EDITION

WITH
ILLUSTRATIONS

GOLD
BOOK

FIVE-MINUTE
SHORT STORIES

K. R. SANFORD

GOLD
BOOK
of FIVE-MINUTE
SHORTS

Paperback
Edition

K. R. SANFORD

GOLD BOOK: FIVE-MINUTE SHORTS

For information address:
500 W. Hamilton Avenue #110835
Campbell, CA 95008
kenrsanford@gmail.com

ASIN: B088BDKG26

ISBN: 9798643939603

United States of America

TABLE OF CONTENS

The Ghost Painting
On the Subject of Writing
An-Other-Worldly Dream
The Frog Story
Sure Enough
The Speech of the Five Senses
The Vision Quest
The Razor's Edge
The Thread that Binds
Molly Doesn't Party!
The Veil of Infinity
The Warrior Dialogue
Boredom And The Surfer
The Bank Teller's Code
The Iterated Prisoner's Dilemma
To Die For
About the Author

Note to the Reader:

It is critical these days for independent authors such as me to get feedback from my readers. Your comments and suggestions about GOLD BOOK of Five-Minute Shorts are welcome.

Send your emails to: kenrsanford@gmail.com

Take a moment to visit my website at:

www.legions-riddle.com

THE GHOST PAINTING

One morning, like most mornings, I finished my coffee, grabbed my cell phone, put my reading glasses in my pocket, then started for the door.

But this morning something I saw out of the corner of my eye was different. It was not different in any normal sense. It was more mysterious, like the presence of something or someone. It was enough to make me stop and sense my surroundings.

I turned to where I had a painting hanging on the wall. During the first few years I owned it, I discovered the painting was made by a master.

It was a rendering of the landscape fifteen miles from where Mount Saint Helen's blasted 1,000 feet off her summit. The eruption devastated 230 square miles of forests, roads, railways and houses. Everything for eight miles was almost blasted away in an instant. Ash and gas blew 12 miles into the air. Over the next few days an estimated 540 million tons of ash drifted over 2,200 square miles. It settled over seven states.

The artist managed to capture nature's power of what remained one year later. According to the USGA, heat melted nearby glacial ice, then snow mixed with dirt. The debris raced down the mountain at speeds reaching 90 miles per hour. It destroyed everything in its path.

I realized there was something else going on in that painting. At that moment, I paused before heading out the door. It captured me by its power. It sat me down in the chair nearby.

I paused to study the abstract images in the painting. My attention went to the light oak swirl of clouds shaped like the head of an angry bear. It stunned me because the bear looked as if it were alive. The bear's anger was directed at me.

It was obvious the image had mirrored my subconscious. It cut through me to project what I was about to carry into the world that morning. I was a toxin primed to dump on the next victim in my path, like the volcano spewing hot gas and lava.

I have lived with this painting for more than twenty years now. This was the first time it showed me it was capable of a meaningful relationship.

It's kind of funny because about a year and a half ago I gave the painting away. Circumstances changed for my friend, so he returned it. He said, "This painting, well, would be much better off with you. And besides, I don't have a place to hang it that would give it the honor it deserves." I nodded, and noticed my friend's relief when I accepted it back into my custody.

I named it The Ghost Painting because it proved it had a life of its own. And, to this day it continues to wow me with messages when I take the time to look at it.

At those times, I sit and observe the abstract images. I watch as the light plays in the oak mist that would otherwise appear as the husk of Nature still at work.

ON THE SUBJECT OF WRITING

At an annual writer's event, a literary critic of some reputation was kind enough to ask for my opinion. She said, I should explain, "When is a piece of writing perfect?"

An astute question by design, I thought, and subjective to the one who looks at it. I accepted the challenge and did not feel put upon because I hadn't finished looking at her ample tits. I tore myself away from the provocative view and responded.

When a work takes on a life of its own
When a work becomes a reflection for the
reader
When a work makes a call to action
Then it is ready to take part in the world.

Writing is a singular activity, conjured in the sanctity of one's own consecrated space. It is a craft that demands the most intense and vivid of imaginations. And, like all potions, one runs the risk of losing the vitality and vigor of expression.

You need, of course, to recognize every detail in your lover's eyes. Then, when you get yourself all sweaty and worked up for nothing, you find it is true. If you are only trying to melt away those unwanted calories, you can do whatever you want.

In the end, it's about your journey for style, riches and your greatest desires.

I say, keep as close to divinity as you can. After all, as long as you're not pissing-off the gods, you're destined to be a big star —huge in fact.

An-Other-Worldly-Dream

The Dream is an experience based on strong emotions.

I was sitting at a table in a fine restaurant. A lovely young couple sat across the aisle in a small booth made for two. It appeared they were on a speed date. They were having a good time until they began arguing over some point of rule in their meeting. Before I was able to figure out what was going on, the lovely young lady turned and asked if I would care to join them.

I wondered where I would sit. But before I could answer, the well-dressed young man got up. He asked me if I would be kind enough to chaperone his date. It would be for the rest of the evening. Then we would meet later for drinks at the hotel. With the hesitations expected of a middle-aged professional, I agreed.

After a brief goodbye, the young man hurried off leaving the lovely brunette and me to get acquainted.

"I'm Bart," I said. "Bart Johnson."

"Katherine," the young lady replied as she offered me her hand.

I gazed into her dreamy blue eyes. I found an immediate connection: an inviting connection of an exotic untouched world. Without another thought, I reached out and caressed her palm.

She captured me by the charm of her beauty. I pressed my lips against the back of her hand and kissed her with the faintest escape of a warm breath.

I felt my loins give rise. I thought of getting lucky with this sweet young lady. She sparked my urge to pull down her panties and tongue-twirl her fancy like the wings of a butterfly in heat. "Oh my God," I said to myself as I struggled to reign in my primal lusts.

Katherine oozed sexuality accentuating every move on her face. Still, we exchanged the usual pleasantries of polite society. But at last, my curiosity got the better of me which forced me to ask, "What are you into?"

"Oh well," she replied, as a matter of fact. "My favorite positions, things like that?"

"No!" I smiled. She would have told me everything. Now I wanted her more than ever. "I'm sorry, no," I repeated. "I'm curious what game this is you're playing. I mean, you're dressed up, you and your date."

I tried to reply half hoping she would see through my reveries to my true desires of making her moan. I tried at the same time to give the impression of a well-balanced gentleman.

"You're having drinks later in the middle of town at the hotel. It all seems so extravagant and rich," I said, taking a well-needed breath. "And as for me, aren't I a bit out of place in this leather jacket and blue jeans?"

"Shabby sheik, oh no," she replied. "You fit right in. And your cowboy boots are dressy, are they not?" she added with a silky smile and generous red lips.

I acquiesced and agreed about the boots. At length, I said, "Your group has intentions. And, you have objectives, like discovering the character and depth of your date. It looks to me you also have places for safe timeouts."

"Yes," Katherine replied. "Yes, like when you showed up. We can't abandon our date. We can choose an agreeable substitution, like you, to move things along for the group's aim."

"Funny," I replied. "I considered myself lucky at getting hijacked by a beautiful woman with a cause. At all cost, you say. Whatever do you mean? How far do you take that?"

Katherine replied without hesitation. "It's not self-motivated. We all want to move on and find the brightest and best associates and leaders to help our common interests. We are in a feverous search to find the highest forms of intelligence in our fellow humans. I take it your senses got woke up a bit."

"I'll say," I announced. "I experienced some intense visceral sensations."

"You found a good connection, Bart," replied Katherine. "Hang onto it. Something of valuable will come of it."

"Katherine," I rejoined. "Like Shakespeare said: 'We're all players.'"

"What part would you like to play, Bart?" she smiled.

Our eyes locked once again. I felt the desire for an intimate evening. Our minds swirled together for an-other-worldly-dream.

The End

THE FROG STORY

The Frog Story *is a whimsical tale of autonomous leadership written to reach the child within and tantalize the romantic curiosity in us all.*

*Liquid as a mirror
shining in the night
The bright sun of day
turned the sky of night
To a pale powder blue
one fine morning light*

The mist of spring hovered in the scent of the tall trees beside the clear cool waters.

Singing through the mist were the song birds that chased each other from flower to flower. In the shade of the tall trees the bulrushes with their thick grass grew high and evergreen.

The grass was a pale green brush rooted along the shores that swayed from side to side with the slightest of wind.

The bugs would explore the life in the brush. They would smell the sweet blades of grass and race through the pale green brush. They would even land on the reeds and drink from the dew drops in the morning light.

Over the clear cool waters, floating in the middle of the pond, was a single lily pad. Although not alone, there were other lily pads of the same likeness. They floated along the edge of the quiet pond in their quiet shaded woods.

And sitting in the middle of the lily pad was the Most Impressive Frog. He sat content with his strong arms pressed out straight. He held himself upright to see far across to the other side.

On days when the mist blew down from the tall trees, he would explore the depths beneath his lily pad. There were creatures of every kind under his lily pad that would be a sight to behold.

Most of the creatures would be hunting for food or swimming to the outer depths of their watery world. Sometimes they would chase each other. And sometimes they would hide and watch as their watery world floated by.

Other times, the Most Impressive Frog would join with the other frogs. They would hunt for eggs or swallow a nice tasty bug. Or when he was not hungry, he would hop along the sandy shores under the shade of the tall trees.

Most of the time he would sit on his own lily pad. He would watch the green brush along the banks sway from side to side with the slightest of wind.

One day while he was sitting on his lily pad, spying far across to the other side, he saw something moving in the water. It was something he had not seen before. And that something was coming straight for him.

It was moving closer and closer, and it was getting bigger and bigger. It looked like it could be the beak of a duck or the nose of a water snake, but he was not sure.

Finally, he saw it was nothing at all but the nose of a girl and a frog girl at that. And if that wasn't enough, she had the same likeness as him.

He thought, "I don't know what to do or even what to think." But when she lifted her head out of the water everything changed.

His head went into a spin for she was the most beautiful frog girl he had ever seen. And that messed his mind way far gone because she had turned him into a fairy prince.

He gave his head a shake. Then, looking down, he saw to his amazement he still had his frog legs. He still had his frog feet and he still had his strong frog arms.

It seemed he was not a fairy prince after all. He only felt like he was a fairy prince. And as everyone knows, facts and feelings are two different things.

So he said, "Hello, Beautiful Frog Girl."

And she said, "Hello, Impressive Frog."

And he said, "What are those bubbles coming up from behind you, Beautiful Frog Girl? Do you have someone down there with you?"

"Oh no, I only wish," she said as she wiggled her finger at something on the back of her head. "I added a little ginger root to my diet this morning and it gave me the wind something awful."

"Ah, don't worry about it, Beautiful Frog Girl," he said. "It could happen to anybody. I remember once when it happened to me, and not too long ago, either.

I was swimming along, right here in this very same spot. I was minding my own business when I felt this mud moving in the pit of my stomach. And the pressure, you know, was beginning to get a bit much.

So I began thinking, what should I do? Then, at that moment, bubbles blew up around me and went right in my face.

Of course, I kept on swimming. That way, I could shake it off like any other thing I couldn't explain."

So she said, "Yes, that's brilliant," with a quizzical look in her eye. "You know," she continued, with her finger held straight up.

"I have to say, listening to the way you tell that story, I am sure I know you. Yes, I'm positive. And I know who you are. As a matter of fact, I would know you anywhere."

"Well," he replied, "I'm sure you think you do, only I haven't been anywhere. I was born right here and here is where I have been."

"No!" she shrieked, "It's the other world, the world of dreams. I have known you in my dreams," she said as a matter of fact.

"Hmm, well there is something I would like to say about that," he said.

"Oh, what's that?" she replied.

So he whispered in her ear, "Ribbit-Ribbit."

"Oh!" she exclaimed. "That was what my dream was about. Ribbit-Ribbit."

And they might have lived 'happy ever after,' except this story isn't over yet. What happened next was beyond all imagination. True things often were in frog stories. Well, this is what happened.

She said to the Most Impressive Frog, "Is there room enough for two on your lily pad?"

He looked around and before he could answer, she climbed up there with him. Then she tried to make him play leapfrog right there on his lily pad in the middle of the pond.

He said, "You are beginning to bug me Frog Girl. I mean, you are starting to bug me."

And she said, "So, I'm not Beautiful Frog Girl anymore? I'm only Frog Girl?"

He said, "I didn't have that dream you had, and what you say is a bit too much for me."

She said, "Do you want me to go?"

And he said, "Do you see those lily pads along the banks in the shade of the tall trees? Go there and you will find the one in your dreams. Then, I can look far to the other side on my own lily pad."

She agreed and swam away. And he sat on his lily pad content by himself in the middle of the pond looking far to the other side.

And they did live happy ever after. Almost.

Because after a time, when emotions settled down a bit, The Frog Girl drank from the dew drops on the bulrushes.

Then, when it was late, she would swim over to The Most Impressive Frog's lily pad. There, they would play 'Secret Leapfrog' until the morning light.

For after all, he had the biggest lily pad in the entire pond. And that right there is what changed Frog Girl back into Beautiful Frog Girl. So you see, after a time, even in this pond, they can live happy ever after. And that brings us to the end of—

The Frog Story

"Ribbit"

Sure Enough

The shriek of a young boy cut through the afternoon air like a jagged knife. "If I told you once I've told you twice!" screamed a woman.

"I won't do it again, momma, stop, please stop, momma," pleaded the boy.

"You'll pull your weight under this roof!" growled the voice of a man.

The boy shrieked again. This time the sound was deeper, of real pain, the kind that a body would not forget.

I held up my fist for the men to hold their horses. I could see across the road to the front of a quaint cottage where the screen door had sprung open. A boy in a torn t-shirt and blue jeans came running out onto the lawn. He marched toward a stump at the side of the road up ahead. He never once looked back to see if he was being followed. I got the idea this was an occurrence that had formed into some acceptable habit.

We moseyed up to where the boy was sitting on the stump. As I pulled up on the reins I looked over at his torn t-shirt and bruises. I gave the kid an inquiring nod. He made no hesitation. He looked me straight in the face and said, "Some days are like that, Mister, sure."

The southern snap in the boy's voice and his straightforward manner brought me up tall in the saddle. "Yes, some days *are* like that, young man," I replied, "Sure enough." The corner of his lip turned up in a weary smile.

I looked back at the men who'd felt the sting of trouble of their own over the past few days and that was also sure. I turned back to the boy and nodded, touching the brim of my hat with a casual salute. Then we turned on the road and went on our way. I didn't know it at the time but I would meet up with that young man some ten years later. Then it would be a real battle over a matter of life and death.

We were all tired and downright hungry. It was getting late. Still, some things do come to every man, woman and child. When I looked back a second time, I could see the men were thinking the same thing, each in their own way of course, and that was also *sure enough*.

The End

THE SPEECH OF THE FIVE SENSES

Excerpt from INTERSTELLAR

"What do you want from me?" said Walters.

"Your cooperation," replied Balrug.

"Well, I'm not going to cooperate," said Walters.

"Oh good, that means you can listen," retorted Balrug.

"You are wasting your time, Balrug. I don't plan on being around for you or anyone else. And for that matter, I don't care to share this universe with anyone."

"I can understand why you would feel that way." Balrug changed his voice. "Let us worry about that, Jim. Since you have proven your decisions to be unsound, we are going to show you why that is. Then we are going to give you some tools so you can live by yourself in peace and quiet, how's that?"

"I have made up my mind, so piss off old man."

Balrug and Marco took a seat next to the viewer and watched the activity outside on the runway.

"Where, where's the place you're talking about?" asked Walters.

Marco turned from the viewer. "You talkin' to us, Walters?"

"Yes, Walters is talking to us," said Walters.

"Is it talking to us in the third person, is it?" chided Balrug.

"I don't know what you're talking about. I can't move."

"He doesn't want to leave us, does he?" goofed Marco.

"I'm stuck goddam it!"

"She shot you up with some crazy medicine shit, so lay there and relax."

"Who?"

"Who? Where have you been? Chris, you know the one in the white coat and tits."

"Oh yeah," said Walters lustfully. "I'd like to pound her bacon."

Marco chuckled, "I bet she would let you."

"You think so?"

Marco raised his hands in disbelief. "I thought you were planning to kill yourself. Now you want to stick your business end in Hector's new squeeze. I'm very disappointed in you, Walters."

"Oh, I'll pound Hector too. That way I can have two for the price of one."

"Now there is where you better watch your mouth. Hector doesn't have a sense of humor," growled Marco.

Walters fell silent, breathing heavy and moaning. Balrug raised an eyebrow, turning to Marco with a knowing smile. They both sat back and waited for Walters to speak first.

"What's next?" whispered Walters.

"Are you in any pain?" asked Marco.

"No."

"We go through your senses, one by one and activate your presence here and now."

Walters stared at the ceiling for an awkward moment, then turning his head away he replied, "Okay."

Balrug and Marco gave each other a glance of caution. "Okay," said Marco turning to Balrug with an affirming nod. "Listen to the sounds around you. Hear the hum of the work outside, the voices in the corridor. Listen for the growl of the sanitation tank off-gassing. Hear the muffled vibrations of your inner ear trembling from shock."

Walters moaned.

"Jim, may I call you Jim?"

Marco looked to Balrug. Balrug shook his head. "Okay, Mister Walters, move to sight. Look at the texture of the light. Look, don't react. See the shadows on the walls. See the lights that move. Look at the soft lights. Then look at the light that draws your attention. See the colors and nothing else. That's fine.

Okay, now what you feel. Your middle finger, the largest of your five senses. This is reproduction, family your offspring. Feel if you are you hungry? Feel if you are in the moment or in your imagination. Next, test your sense of smell, your olfactory gland. This gland has direct connections with two areas of the brain. They are the amygdala and hippocampus. More than any other sense, smell is what triggers emotional and memory response. It's like when you smell the perfume of a long-lost lover. In your mind you are immediately transported back to that time."

Walters groaned, "I know this."

"Okay good, very good," said Marco. Balrug nodded. Marco continued. "Your sense of taste can give you clues. I remember when I banged myself up like you. I had a coppery taste in my mouth. It warned me of broken bones."

Walters groaned again. Marco watched his body lay still on the table. "Still can't move? The effects of the drug will wear off in a half hour or so."

"What's next?" said Walters.

"Let's recap. We went through the five senses we connect with Nature. When you stretched out your hand you remind yourself of the five senses. This is where you connect to the now . . . the ever changing here and now. This is your real home, the present, where you make things happen, where you are responsible for what you do. In this exercise we stay out of the past and the future. You will end up back in your imagination living like a child. And I know you don't want that. Now, there is more. We will get into that now that our senses are active. Look at me Walters. Another thing, this process will make your autonomy more reliable."

Marco spread his fingers. He moved his palm toward Walters face. He turned over his hand and began curling his little finger. He was forming his fingers one by one into a fist. "This is a point charge," he said, repeating the motion. "Field force; point charge." He repeated the movement several times, gritting his teeth and straining his voice. Each time he built a more intense state of determination. Walters flinched.

Balrug stepped up and smiled. "Allow me this part?" Marco moved aside and Balrug continued. "You are an educated man, Captain Walters."

"I'm not a Captain anymore," said Walters.

"You earned your bars," replied Balrug. "When you have three to five electrons you have a field and a force of electricity. Well, depending on the size of the electrons of course."

"Right, I guess, I'll take your word for it," said Walters laughing.

"What's this? He's laughing at my lecture, Marco."

"Yeah and you've only started," said Marco with a grin.

"So this is also true for photons," Balrug continued. "One photon by itself does not carry an electrical charge. You need a packet of photons to carry an electrical charge to a battery. This is the same for gravity. You need about five gravitons to make a gravitational field. This depends on the density of the massless graviton. This makes a difference with high energy spin."

Walters puckered his lips and was shaking his head.

"You've lost the business at hand, Balrug," said Marco. "May I? We are introducing two other forces that connect us to our universe. Do you follow, Walters?"

"Right, with a field force or point charge," said Walters. "How does that work with people?"

"Usually, after the fact, one sees the result. This is a cautionary note for the farmer. There isn't always instant gratification. Sometimes the application is like planting a seed and you have to wait for the result to mature in season."

Walters laughed, "First, I thought you were going to turn me into a spin dryer, now it sounds like you want me to be a farmer."

"You're not far off," said Marco. "All-the-above actually. Sometimes people need a dictator. Other times people need a democracy, a de-centralized consensus. Onboard a starship, the Captain is the dictator. You don't run a ship by committee."

"No, I see that," said Walters. "I am a military man, Captain. I understand the importance of the chain-of-command."

Marco nodded in agreement. "There are times and places for each," he continued.

"Yes, I see that. Where do we go from here?"

"Right," replied Balrug. "We take one step at a time. We take one moment at a time with all the determination of the Warrior. We are present and accounted for at every moment. This is our infinite direction of purpose."

"This sounds charismatic, Balrug. To what end?" replied Walters.

"To no end, Walters; to no end at all. Here we take the infinite perspective," said Balrug. "You will now have the opportunity to prepare yourself for an advanced state of being. You have the opportunity to evolve the value of your own autonomy. The end is in shaping a better more satisfying identity."

"Okay," said Walters. "You have given me something to think about."

"Sure," replied Balrug, tapping Marco and pointing to the door. Without another word they disappeared out the examination room. They left Walters to his private thoughts.

In the corridor Balrug spoke again. "Do you think he heard anything?"

"If you mean, is he ready to reinvent himself? I would say he doesn't have a snowballs chance in hell. He's not our problem anyway. This is the Emperor's pet project. Let him deal with it. We gave him the speech and that's what we said we would do. The more I'm around Walters the more I want to spit."

"He reminds you of yourself?"

Marco chuckled. "That's possible. Let's go to the cafeteria, I want a couple of those fish tacos Vito keeps talking about."

"Fish tacos," replied Balrug. "That does sound good."

* * * *

THE VISION QUEST

Excerpt from
THE HERO'S JOURNEY

Captain Marco W. Miller turned on his heels. He picked up the crutches off the rail, placed them under the pits of his arms, and hobbled back along the pier. He walked through the sand to the door of the snack shack. He pushed the buzzer on the entry pad and the door hissed open. He stepped inside. The magnavator shot up to the first level of the ship. He stepped out into the hallway and went to his quarters. He lay on his bed staring at the ceiling. He turned over, closed his eyes, and fell into a deep sleep.

Hours later he awoke to a soft white light. The light emerged around his bedchamber. He felt a familiar presence. He stirred and tried to focus on its source but the light drew away. It lifted above him. It formed itself into the brightness of a star. He watched as the star moved higher above his bedchamber.

As the star radiated a soft glow, it draped a translucent veil down around his bed. He lay astonished, fascinated with the beauty of its subtle salutation. The veil closed in and isolated him with the star fixed within the center of his chamber.

He studied the light. Its presence had a life, a feeling, a comfort and an ease within its unifying source. He felt the dimension of time and space slip away from his conscious thoughts. His body felt weightless and he lifted up from the lap of his luxurious bedchamber. The pain in his body and mind began to fall away.

The star moved higher in his quarters. Its light opened through the ceiling of the ship. It rose still higher beyond the ship's upper bulkhead. It traveled up through the dark expanse of space. As the star broke the barriers of the universe's womb, he felt a comfort. He felt the ease of its truss move in unison through his body and his mind. Marco, curious for exploration, relaxed to the invocation of the guiding light.

He moved upward through the beam of veiled light. As he traveled, the presence in the veil stood him upright. He was standing on both feet and the pain within his body had vanished. He traveled beyond the upper bulkhead of the Eagle. He could see below to the charring of Bradley's torpedoes where they had struck the outer hull. He watched as a brown haze enveloped the composite sides of his starship. The haze appeared as a cloud of cosmic dirt. It was the symbol of a galaxy gone astray.

Marco compared his ascended view of the Eagle to the ultra-dimension of the veil. It appeared like a force field. It was a barrier to the cold outer darkness. He placed his hand against the force and felt its substance. It was soft and warm. As he pushed deeper into the veil, a cold resistance warned him of the consequences of his own self will. The more he pushed, the more he felt the cold beyond the force.

He could imagine himself pushing through the veil into the dark unknown. As well, he could imagine himself trapped outside in space, lost with no way back and no return. He had enough miscalculations for one day. The boundaries of his judgment had lapsed too often for any more of his sophomoric tests. He pulled his hand back inside the veil. He surrendered to the hospitality of his exploration.

At that instant, he watched the brilliance of the star lead to an upper place beyond his universe. The star was traveling at terrific speed. He looked around and saw he was on a course through the outer cosmos, racing beyond the parameters of light. He was moving in a direction leading far into the unknown. His body grew frail, yet powerful.

His mind became unencumbered, his thoughts began to streamline. He was holding to his memories with a single thread.

His last memories only moments ago had vanished. He expected the darkness to cover him up. He felt a renewing, like a new beginning and a new transformation.

As he looked at his arms and legs, he noticed his clothes begin a transformation. His coat and slacks changed to a finer material. His clothes morphed to a radiant blue fabric of no seams or wrinkles. They fashioned infinite reason by a tailor of immortal understanding.

He looked up within the veil to where he saw the star had stopped. The star set itself in place and held itself on top as if subsisting from a nest. It sent veils of light upon their journey to a concert with its young. It was a place that appeared to Marco as the end of his lifelong journey. Its final resting place.

Marco moved still higher through the veil. He came closer to the star. He raced forward to a place of primordial existence. He grew more and more uncertain of the star's true intended purpose. He could not help desire the power of its brilliance. Yet he could not help admire its authority to divide the darkness from the light. He could not desire its place at the top of its infinite nest. And he would not desire a share of its unique and mighty power. His mind quickened and he sensed its true intentions. His journey had corrected by an energy that went far beyond him. Even more, his journey had corrected from a design that had established before time.

Marco was not prepared, not well enough to take its place. That would be the dimension of unimaginable demise. He did not know or understand its symbolic meaning, only he was certain the star was not his home.

Marco began the deceleration in his journey. He continued moving toward the great star, indeed a great and wondrous star. It had journeyed through the cosmos. Marco was not at one with the greatness of its brilliance. He did not comprehend its composition, but strange as it may seem, he felt born within its source. He moved closer and closer until finally, fear seized him at his core. He determined in his mind, and by the sheer might of his will, he would turn from this thing he was not. Then, at that same moment, he slowed in his ascent until he stopped.

He was standing on solid ground, secure in the veil of soft white light. He took a deep breath. Marco looked to his right and saw a mirror. The mirror was set in a gold frame of French provincial. It was from the fourteenth-century Earth. It was an odd mirror, thought Marco, for being way out here in the far-flung reaches of space. He tested the mirror to see if it gave the reflection of him. It was, in fact, the perfect reflection of a perfect face with perfect skin. It had the perfect nose and the perfect features of a man. Then, as he examined the eyes, upon close and careful inspection, he discovered they were his own. And what was stranger yet, he surmised, was that his hair had been combed with perfection. As he studied the miracle of his perfect hair, a hat appeared resting on his head with the fine exactness of a dream. The hat was that of a prince, he deduced, and it was okay with no one around. Besides, he did not fear or care. How could it matter? How could it matter after he had traveled the full depth of the universe?

Marco looked beneath to the framework of the mirror to where he saw a golden knob. He put his hand on the knob and gave it a turn. The mirror moved back and a door opened. It opened out from the veil into another compelling dimension.

He looked into this new dimension and saw it was a fine place. He saw a floor he recognized. It had the same substance he found in the Lord Legion's temple. Marco was not shocked or surprised, and yet he stood in the doorway in wonder. He wondered at the familiar immortal construction. He wondered at the flat open portal that lay before him.

It was a launch pad to anywhere he could imagine. He stepped out of the veiled corridor and walked across its surface. He walked until he came to the edge. He looked over. There were no stars extending a tiny universe as the Lord Legion's Temple. Likewise, there was no dome overhead with the intelligent life of the Emperor. There were no walls of gold-scaled armor. There was no temple of cerebral convolutions. There was only the glazed floor of transparent gold.

Marco continued along its edge to where a rise of three steps fashioned at a corner outcrop. The steps, constructed of the same immortal substance as the floor, were unbroken. It was the expression of an untraceable builder. He mounted the first step, then the second. At the third he waited. He looked out to the deep void of space and saw only stars. No moving objects were in the distance to absorb his isolation. No moving starships were below him to witness his occurrence. There was only the black abyss below and the stars.

The stars, like all other stars, were in the expanse of their own spacetime. He waited for a voice, a voice that would grant him an acquaintance. He waited for a familiar voice, a voice that did not come. Marco did not so much expect the adoration of the universe to launch celebration of his arrival. But as he turned to carry on his exploration, he saw a figure. A ghost-like apparition. Still, Marco was not surprised or in fear of his life. He was now pleased to see a being standing on the same immortal floor as he. Things were looking up, he thought. Then, the apparition motioned with outstretched arm. Marco looked to see four spirits sitting around a table—a table he did not see before the appearance of the figure. He gazed in veneration upon this new audience.

Marco recognized the spirits as the archetypes of the ancients. They were the four spirits with bodies of beasts. The spirits confronted him as if judging his performance. Each held a separate but equal perspective in their faces. One possessed the face of a lion. The other, the face of an eagle. The next, a face of an ox, and the other had the face of a man. Each face had its own separate and unique personality and powers. They made their perspective clear in the different directions they faced. They instructed Marco to the vast reservoir of their powers. The four spirits showed him the thread that bound the will of their hearts and minds. The thread bound them in a unifying demonstration of their purpose.

Marco listened to the expressions of the beings. He replied with a posture of receptive affirmation. The four spirits acknowledged the will of their purpose through telepathic utterance. They had opened themselves to Marco. They made themselves known in their innermost thoughts. They transmitted their faculties and capacities, talents and intentions, gifts, aspirations and desires. He experienced their message and the significance of its depths in the whole of his body, mind, and spirit. He had gathered and understood the fullness of their enlightened message. He knew them as created from the hand of time.

Marco reflected on the totality of their significance. He turned and gazed upon the guiding figure behind him. The figure, Infinite in its being, beckoned with the offer of its hand.

Marco stepped closer in an attempt to know the intent of the Infinite. The Infinite held him back with the power of its compassion so great that Marco froze where he stood. In that instant, Marco received a telepathic utterance to: *Hold where he stood.* This is the distance established by the unifying spirit.

There in that moment, he understood the guiding friendship of the Infinite. The Infinite again impressed upon Marco that it was a fellow traveler. He could not embrace him at that moment in any closer approximation. Marco, aware of the reverent power of the limits, complied. As he did, he recharged with a quality that he accepted.

Marco experienced an invigorating essence emerging in his being. He was conscious of the fact his experience increased the permanency of his life. He *saw* he could take in and *be* the quality of what he lived as if it were the gift of universal power. The power was far beyond his self-made universe. The essence revitalized his spirit. Its quality was the same as the four archetypes of the ancients.

He grew more and more solid, and felt more and more the fiber of his surroundings. He could *see* with new sensations. He could understand its dynamics and intentions, its magnificence and importance.

Marco was eager for his next lesson in infinite indoctrination. He looked to the Infinite for a newer and still greater revelation.

The Infinite guided Marco's eyes to the starry expanse of space. He looked to where a star surged above all others in its brightness and independence. The star dislodged itself from its position. It drew forward on a course to where Marco stood with the Infinite. As the star drew closer, it evolved from its single point of light. It evolved to a massing of clouds rolling forward through space.

As the clouds charged in, Marco's body began to tremble. He could hear their thunder roaring and he could see the clouds abounding. The roaring thunder quickened every cell in his being. He welcomed the celestial drama unfolding before him. Then, as the morning light brings calm for a bright new day, the clouds stopped in front of Marco.

They cleared away their misty cover. Marco could see the spire-capped turrets and dazzling rows of rooftops. He could see enchanted courtyards and cobbled streets of gold. He could see the clouds surrounding castle walls and inside he could see a beautiful city. Above the beautiful city, stars appeared that gave their light as bright as day. The beautiful city was great and built with flawless grace of days gone by.

Inside the city were lands of rolling hills with a river flowing through the center. The castle nestled within the city walls and beside the flowing river.

Marco turned to the Infinite to inquire about the purpose of the astronomic spectacle. The Infinite impressed within Marco that he was being offered a perpetuating option. Marco saddened because, although no words were spoken, he knew the choice he would make. He would either enter ultimate contentment and arrive in a place where dreams come true, or return to his ship with his own separate and unique lifelong destination.

That destination was the mission for building value in his own character. He would commit to that choice for when his time in mortality expired. It would be his most important venture, but one that would win a victory for himself and civilization.

To do that would mean living as a mortal once again. Marco would live in a high-maintenance body for an unspecified length of time. But after that he could return through the veil of soft white light and accept his place with dignity. He would be deserving of a sphere of influence like the Emperor Lord Legion.

Marco knew he must leave the beautiful city in the clouds with its rolling hills and vivid splendor. And most of all, he would lose his sense of connected fellowship with all he had surveyed. He felt it worthy of himself to return through the dirt and the troubled confusion of the universe. He knew he could have that infinite life at that very moment. But as he thought, he made his decision. He would set his infinite life aside and take up the challenge of the ages. This, he thought, would be his own answer to the Emperor Lord Legion's most difficult of riddles.

What is everyone's?
And what is no one's
And has the power to generate a universe?

Marco knew upon his return to his universe he could call upon the stars if that was what he desired.

The Infinite bid Marco farewell. Its mission was complete and its place was with the spirits of the stars. Marco was again saddened. He would separate from the Infinite and the beautiful city for a short time. But the revelation was more than enough for the journey that lay ahead.

As the city in the clouds lifted away, Marco descended back to the Eagle. He watched in amazement as the city disappeared from sight.

The stars that gave the city their bright illumination shined one last time in unison. Their unbroken goodbye would be the power to bring them back together. Marco looked on. His heart leapt in his chest. Then, as if a silent call went out, one third of all the stars in the celestial theater fell away after the great city.

Marco felt a great loss. He did not realize their presence had the conscious power to make him feel the way he did.

As the stars left him far behind, he began to lose his insights and the ability to speak without the use of words. His instinctive knowledge of the universe faded from his memory. Marco felt disadvantaged. Still, he had his experience, and that was certain enough. What else he would keep from the power of the vision only time would tell.

Then, as he held the vision clear within his mind's eye, the words of the Emperor Lord Legion came ringing in his ears. It gave him courage. He would *know,* when he heard *the suns of thunder.* Marco heard *the sons of thunder* as he had seen the clouds rolling with magnificent sublime. Now he *knew* what he would do with the length his time.

* * * *

THE RAZOR'S EDGE

When I was young, I was curious about a great many things. Looking back, my curiosity was normal for someone my age. I didn't care for things like bugs or snakes or even puppies. I suppose because puppies aren't useful for anything like a dog that can sit or come when you call it. I leaned toward things that could do something for me, like a hammer or a bike. I liked things that had a reason or at least a mystery to uncover. One thing in particular was the jewelry box on the top of my father's dresser.

One day when no one was around, my curiosity got the better of me. I fashioned a method of reaching the top of my father's dresser. I started by pulling out the bottom drawer. Then I would pull out the drawer on top of that, but not as far as the first. I decided I would pull it only far enough to make a step. I did the same to the next so I had a stairway high enough to reach the jewelry box on top. You see, I was blind with curiosity of what hid inside the box.

If I got caught in my mother and father's bedroom it would mean a whipping. The kind of whipping that would leave marks. If I got caught with my hand in the jewelry box, it would be worse. More than my worst nightmare. But no, that didn't stop me.

When I opened the box, I saw a knife out of many that caught my eye. It was a heavy black knife with two blades that folded inside. It was the one you would play mumblety-peg with. At first, I picked it up and looked at it. Then I pulled out the larger of the two blades. It pulled out easy and locked in place with a fine click.

I climbed down off the dresser and onto the floor so I could look at the knife in closer detail. I began pulling at the second smaller blade only to have it snap back onto my fingers. I didn't have the calluses on my hands like I do today. The blood was dripping down my fingers and onto my hand. It seemed the blood was everywhere now on both hands.

Finally, I pulled the blade off my fingers and walked across the hallway to the bathroom to wash it off. I wrapped a Kleenex around my cut fingers and walked back across the hall to my father's dresser. I was able to put the knife back in the jewelry box without panic. Then I closed the drawers to the dresser, switched off the light, and left the room.

I didn't realize how sharp that knife was until I was much older. Someone had kept the edge of that blade as sharp as a razor. It turned out the knife was not my father's; it was my mother's.

My mother was an only child from the age of twelve when her father died in a gunfight at a downtown hotel. Her father, my grandfather, was a known associate of the Chicago Outfit.

This was also normal because during prohibition the big hotels had a speakeasy for its best customers. At the time it was considered rude not to allow the Outfit the business of supplying the hotel with their finest liquor.

* * * *

THE THREAD THAT BINDS

Excerpt from
THE HERO'S JOURNEY

If the thread that binds is so,
let it be without a doubt!
Fuming from his nostrils
his jaw was set.
His eyes flamed red of burning coals
that cut broad paths through black of the
night.
Then, searching like the lightning trace
Defying life to show its face
Thought, mortals' plans will fall to waste
Then shuns to think his own disgrace
A sigh he breathes with deep embrace

Truth proves itself with trust in grace
And the motions of the waves moved on
The pier stood sound in celestial song
Then looking to the stars, he mused
And wished a place among them
But was sobered by those specks of light
Now filling the bellows of the sky
That vault of black
And his destiny awaits him
Out beyond the shimmer of the horizon
Where he saw the ocean had its own
message
Its voice was deep
But he grew tired of these incoming
thoughts
Life was all around him
Then his thoughts dissipated like the mist off
a breaking swell for he was overwhelmed.

* * * *

MOLLY DOESN'T PARTY!

The best gifts live among us every day. They are often unassuming. They are not missed until they are gone. These are the gifts that surprise us. They perform selfless acts of courage. And they make noble sacrifices without giving thought of the consequences to themselves.

I say this because I often think of a dog I used to know. Her name was Molly. She lived and worked in a construction yard with a small pack of dogs in Silicon Valley. Her job was to keep thieves and vandals from doing harm to the equipment.

She was a medium size dog who seemed to get on well with everyone. She didn't look like the feared Pit-Bull. Her head was smaller, almost delicate with a slight physique and gentle disposition.

If a stranger would happen into the yard, she would stop what she was doing and stare, as if to say, "Who are you? What do you need?" Cocking her head to one side, she would study the stranger's body language and keep a polite distance. If the reaction from the stranger was good, she would drop her head and wag her tail. If the reaction was not good, she would immediately stiffen and give a warning, "Woof." She gave one woof and that was it. This gave time for the other dogs to arrive while she advanced toward the intruder.

Some days I would stop by the yard to say hello. She would always remember who I was. She would walk over and welcome me.

Many times, I would be sitting in a chair inside the office discussing details of a project. She would make a point of coming over and laying her head on my knee, then look up at me with those please, please pet me eyes. I would whisper to her, "I am not going to pet you if you keep looking at me that way." But that would only egg her on even more. She would thump her tail on the floor.

After that, I would reach out and scratch her neck and talk to her. She seemed to love that more than anything, even if I had food. Of course, she got the food. It's that she wasn't a pig about it. She loved the intimate communication and the soft touch.

When it was time to get back to business, she would recognize the change in the tones of the voices. She would trot off or lie on the floor until things got a little less intense.

One day, I walked into the yard and found the worker's kids playing under the large covered patio. This was usual for midday. But I didn't see the big German Shepard running around or locked in his cage, and that was a relief. Rex was a pain in the ass.

He would try to dominate, or what we humans call bully, everyone and everything in the yard. He was a real sociopath. He would not stop jumping on people until he got a forceful kick in the chest or got locked in his cage.

I asked where Rex was and one of the girls said, "He's dead!"

This sounded amusing so I inquired, "Oh," thinking someone finally got fed-up with his bullshit and shot him. "What happened?"

"Molly killed him," she said.

"Why did Molly kill Rex?" I asked, wondering if Molly was alright.

One of the girls stepped in and said, "Rex jumped on Molly and tried to do this." She thrust her hips back and forth in a humping motion.

I understood what she meant so I replied, "Because of that?"

The girl was about ten years old and very sweet. She put her hands on her waist and twisted her hip out to one side. With a look of disgust on her face she exclaimed, "Molly doesn't party!"

Molly, as it happened, ripped Rex's throat out without injury to herself. To keep Molly safe, the owner of the company took her to his ranch in San Martin, California. There she lived out her days with the family and the other dogs on the vast manicured lawns. Molly, a black, English Terrier-Pitbull died of natural causes in the spring of 2012.

Rest in Peace, Molly

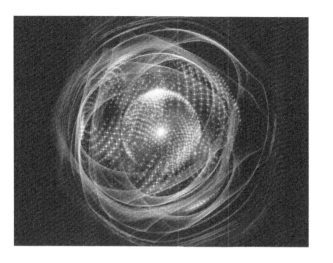

THE VEIL OF INIFNITY

'Pandora's Box' 1928
Performed by the Brilliant Silent Film Star
and Dancer, Louise Brooks, 1906 - 1985

This Classic Film was Later Banned by
Adolph Hitler as 'Degenerate Art'

"We don't know what's going on in the
multiverse," said Admiral Halsted.

"Yes, we do," replied the Emperor. "We know to apply ourselves and realize our most valued gift."

"That's easy for you to say," said Halsted. "You are multidimensional. I am limited by time, and that time has its limits as well."

"There can be a fallacy for thinking at the speed of light, Admiral," said the Emperor. "The Universe does not limit itself to a time constant. There is an advantage for those in the executive files of a multidimensional highway. Wormholes are not for sending starships from one side of universe to the other. This happens at great risk to the life-force and to the ship. No, it's for access to other dimensions. This is a much safer process for travel and for guarding valuables. You are the key. You, I mean, Admiral, the individual life-force."

"I am not the only one at a disadvantage, My Lord. This technology is beyond most of us here."

"I am well aware of that," said the Emperor. "Look at this project as a theme park. Better still, see this as an amusement park for grown-ups. Allow my introduction to the theme. Here is an opportunity to give the adventurous a profitable challenge. It's like a new scene in a movie production. Let's call it an E ticket to the Future; the future that requires a type four body like myself. This, of course, leaves you to take part in your present form."

"Are we to recombine somehow and enter another dimension without corrupting our DNA? I'm not that naïve, Emperor," said the Admiral.

"Try not to cloud your judgment with fears of the unknown, Admiral Halsted. I do welcome your comments. They are important and worth addressing. We are under no time constraints here, only let's understand, time is of the essence on this space station. So save political demagoguery for later."

"I wasn't—"

Halsted got interrupted by the Amedans on an intercept course. They flanked him in his chair. They held their positions midair the moment he stopped speaking.

"Fine, that's fine boys," whispered the Emperor. "Mark Kiterage, CEO of the Triumph Corporation will make a presentation. He will speak on the ultimate in virtual reality, our E-ticket to the future. Mister Kiterage," he said. Legion offered Kiterage the floor with an open hand.

Kiterage took center stage in his iridescent suit. With a dramatic sweep of his arm, he pointed to the super highway outside the observation windows. "Spacetime of all multiverses is not a river like most assume," he said. "It's more like a cube with an executive file that allows entrance to any spacetime you chose.

Let's say a type four wants to control the spacetime from outside the cube. And he wants to control the entanglement of spacetime within the cube. Who will prevent the type four from controlling all the dimensions of the cube? Unless one can get there with a type four body, everything is subject to the originator or controller. A scalable type four body is needed to manipulate the multiverse. If you can bypass all iterations up to the very last one, you will secure all iterations. Infinite conscience existence becomes defendable, this added to not owning the information within the self-aware being. The structure of your *infinite-self,* reorganizes as an autonomous universe." Kiterage took a sip of his beverage to give the guests a moment to digest the information, then continued.

"The trick is to use a relative power source equal to the target continuum. Then, open a portal for the transmission of your payload."

An officer with the insignia of the atom over a starship on his lapel stood up and asked, "Is there enough spacetime for many controllers to establish a network before bifurcation?"

"Yes, Robert," said Kiterage. "The experiment is proven so when you get there life will be there with you."

Robert spoke again. "The experiment will test when a second cube is able to sustain intelligent life?"

Kiterage replied. "We start by perfecting wormholes for the safe transmission of intelligent mass. Signals containing information will get sent by drones and then robots. We help neutrino showers with seeding so the cube will self-sustain life-forms.

This scenario takes place unbeknown to the biologics predestined condition. In other words, evolution does not suspect it is being used in service of the cube. The process is a wonderful engine for the conservation of energy. The process includes the information needed for the self to reorganize itself. This last point is for the instinct of survival within self-aware beings."

Admiral Halsted raised a hand. He questioned from his chair. "Can the soul get lost during transmission? Will death occur, one might ask? This is the obvious safety question on everyone's mind."

"What risks could we be facing?" rejoined Kiterage. "I get that. We had this discussion involving almost every species in the Universe. Impressions came from entities in parallel dimensions. We called this our Pandora's Box scenario.

The mind entangles within a matrix. The matrix behaves like a wave-form in a shell game shuffle, or the Three Card Monty, the slide of hand. When the playing field is at the macro landscape, energy escapes at the speed of light. The speed of light constant stabilizes the process for the collapse of the waveform. The true position of the frequency of the event cannot get known. This, of course, is Heisenberg's classic uncertainty principle.

To simplify, consider the yin-yang dynamic. When light reaches darkness its tail-end slips away. Darkness evades capture ad infinitum. This creates an infinite reality for existence in a fourth dimension. This also is a metaphor where your conscience mind finds itself. The mind wants a boundary within the safe harbor of spacetime. This is a virtual reality scenario, or game theory. Our scientists can use this landscape for some exciting experimentation."

"And your test subject is a probe then drones and robots," said the Admiral.

"That's right, that's right. We call this process, 'Piercing the Vail of Infinity,'" said Kiterage, making a dramatic hand wave motion, "unless the unforeseeable happens."

High Ruler Lao hovered before the Emperor. "My Lord, the infirmary has Walters. Do I send him back to the Mastodon?" he said.

"No, this is perfect," said Legion. "Ask Marco to work with him. I have an idea."

"Very well, My Lord," said Lao. "What idea?"

"We can use him like a guinea pig and accelerate him through the machine, then convert him into energy. But that doesn't mean the guys in medical have to treat him any different than any other patient. I don't like it when people get singled out and used for some special reason or another. Okay, Lao, and you can tell him I said that."

"Very good, My Lord," said Lao. "I'll let him know how you feel," He raced away in a flash of light. He sailed between the two sentries guarding the entrance.

Grantham stood next to Legion. He turned and gave Legion a wild-eyed look.

"What? I was kidding," said Legion. "That psychopath Lao will go down to medical and tell Walters exactly what I said. Then he'll tell him, he's not getting any privileges and will most likely be dead first thing in the morning."

Grantham shook his head. "You are incorrigible," he said.

"I know," he replied, smiling from ear to ear. He broke into a belly laugh. Kiterage turned from his Q and A as if inviting the Emperor to let them in on the joke.

"Aren't you done yet?" said the Emperor. "Come on, Kiterage, let's go check out the babes."

THE WARRIOR'S DIALOGUE

*"I'm sorry. I don't know why nobody told you
how to unfold your love.
While my guitar gently weeps"* – George
Harrison 1968

After more kills than one cares to recall, says the Warrior, one begins to reflect on things other than one's duty to one's homeland. This is a work for an infinite connection, a perspective beyond the mortal condition.

You might be unclear about your part here. Still, in your rest you see the eyes of the dead haunt you in your dreams. They stare back with blank faces wanting what they do not know.

But you know all too well what they seek.

You think this day has come sooner than you expected.

The proximity of your mortality comes closer and closer.

You begin to feel the pressing of your thoughts.

You know the time has come to give account.

You are confident you possess the right value to meet your enemies.

You need only enough value to make your enemies become your allies.

You need only find enough common ground for your leadership to flourish.

Failure to supply those foreshortened lives with adequate measure, or failure to follow through with your leadership would show your lack of real purpose. This is where your life would get reduced to the baseness of vanity and the striving afterwind. So an Infinite Connection becomes Your Ally.

Here is where one lays down the illusion of the Eternal.

Here is where one begins the journey of internalizing the inherent Forces of Nature.

Here is where we harness the potential powers of the Universe.

Here is where we take up the gauntlet of the Warrior one more time.

Here is where we get to the mission at hand.

* * * *

BOREDOM AND THE SURFER

Boredom comes in waves. Boredom is periodic and it can stifle your performance. The trick is understanding the cavernous distraction of boredom. It's like the day of the surfer.

The surfer will set up their position before the wave breaks. They know the work of catching the wrong wave can get exhausting and waste energy. It takes effort to paddle back out and pick up another wave.

Once you do catch a wave, it lifts you up. You are on alert. It's exhilarating and you don't want to let it go. You can snake from side to side to slow your run so the wave gets underneath your board. The technique makes you climb higher on the wave. Now you've got a mountain of water to work with. You ride the wave for all it is worth.

Your ride was a good one and you head for the crest of the wave to kick out. You glide to a spot that's good and you hop off. You are ready to go back out and try it again. So you do.

After flipping the board over a couple times, and you finish selling your soul to the god Poseidon, you paddle back out through the first line of breakers. The waves get bigger the farther out you go. You are going to have to work at it. If you lose your board, you will need to pull it in and climb back on. You're glade to find your ankle line is still attached.

It's exhausting but you have made it through to the yawn before the next set closes-out. You paddle over to the right place to set and wait.

It's a quiet time. It's a time to catch your breath. You are feeling tired. The waves have beat some of your life out of you. So you let a few good waves go by until you are done resting. You feel the water. It's beginning to get cold. You are still waiting for a wave to come to where you set yourself.

It looked like a good spot at the time. Your mind wonders and you think you may have seen a fin poke out of the water from the corner of your eye. You turn your head and you're sure you saw something drop back down, most likely a seal, or maybe a fucking shark. You say it out load. Good thing no one is around, otherwise they will know you love to swear, especially at fucking sharks. You can hear them all now. "Oh yeah, the surfer, the one you can hear swearing from the cliffs. He was eaten by a shark, you know." There is something comical about that, but I just don't know what.

Anyway, back to the swearing. Swearing is liberating. It is an opportunity to take back your power from a world that wants to put you in a box of their sensibilities.

It was John Adams who said something about Freedom of Speech: If you suppress any voice, it will come back and bite you sooner or later. He went on to say: The

Constitution of the United States is not only a document to rule a nation but a document to rule your own soul.

John Adams lived to be ninety years old. If only we, in this day, could be so lucky. He was a man on a mission. He raised a son, John Quincy Adams, who also became President of the United States. John Quincy carried on the same principles of liberty as his father.

* * * *

THE BANK TELLER'S CODE
(PERSONAL VALUE)

A man walked into a bank. He went to the teller's window and said, "I'd like to cash this check." He laid it on the counter and waited for the teller.

The teller examined the check and said, "Everything looks in order, sir. I just need your signature on the back." She turned over the check and pointed to the line across the top.

The man replied with a request of his own. "My word is good whether I sign the check or tell you it is good. So this is my check. It is good. And I'd like you to give me the cash."

The teller looked the man up and down, then said, "One moment, Sir. Let me get the manager of the bank."

When the teller returned, she asked the man to follow her to the manager's office.

After the man was greeted by the bank manager, the manager dismissed the teller and closed the door. He asked the man why he was not willing to endorse the check. The man told the manager the same thing he told the teller.

At that moment, the bank manager gave the man a quick lesson from the school of hard knocks. He sent the man a haymaker square across on the mandible nerve of his jaw. The man staggered and nearly fell over. After that, the man didn't say a word. He turned over the check on the manager's desk and signed it. Then he walked out of the manager's office and laid it once again in front of the bank teller.

The teller looked at the signature and said, "What changed your mind?"

The man replied, "I haven't had it explained to me like that before."

She said, "He does have a way with words. Not to worry, Sir, the details of your transactions are safe with us. At this bank, all your valuables are treated with the strictest security."

The man smiled and was convinced.

The moral of the story is in the Institution of Trust.

The bank teller knows the code. It is to her value to look to a prosperous future.

The bank teller was promoted and given a raise based on time and trust. In a bank, a lot of money is handled every day. More than that, valuable information gets secured in various depositories. In the wrong hands, devastating harm can occur to the customer's accounts. Having an employee who can be trusted to keep information safe makes that employee a valuable asset, like real property in a robust market. They are worth a raise and a promotion. It may seem like a little thing, but I like what Bob Dylan once said,

"If you are going to live an outlaw life, you better be honest, because those people will kill you."

THE ITERATED PRISIONER'S DILEMMA
Naval Ravikant
AngelList Founder
(Cheaters in the Ecosystem)

"In game theory, people play the game over and over. It is beneficial to cooperate with the players because you know you will play with them again. When a new person comes in the game, the rewards can be huge. You can make twenty million to fifty million and win then leave. The temptation is to cheat. They want it now."

"Whenever someone comes in as a newcomer, you have to decide if this person is someone I want to know. Is this person someone I will be doing business with a decade from now? If not, you have to be wary of what they are offering."

When asked, "How do you know if you want to do business with someone a decade from now?" Naval replied, "First thing is: Do you like them? Second is: Do you trust them? You have to pick that up in little ways. References obviously matter. How considered and considerate are they about things? Are they over-optimizing? Are they fighting for a tiny piece? This means, they are over-reaching. Therefore, they are not ready to do business with you at this time."

Note to investors:

There are exceptions to every rule. And there are many exceptions to generalities. In every case, it is the accepted convention to complete your *Due Diligence* before investing time and monies.

To Die For

Identifying a weakness is critical for securing Good Health. If you can't identify what's wrong, you can't fix it. I will give you an example.

I was getting off an airplane at the Rapid City Regional Airport in South Dakota. I needed to get my pickup truck so I could take it back to California. Later that evening, I felt something was wrong. I was feeling a bit under the weather. I suspected it was something I picked up on the airplane, or it was another onset of a recurring blood infection. I took 500 mg of Cephalexin because the symptoms persisted.

The next morning I felt better. I gassed-up the pickup and headed out on I-80 to California. Two days later I was driving through Salt Lake City, Utah with a high fever and not enough sense to stop and get checked out. If I could make it to Reno, Nevada I would be in more familiar territory. That was my thinking.

Thirty miles later I was seeing double and suffering from dehydration. Desperate for relief, I pulled into the only store and gas station on that stretch of highway. I managed to turn-off the engine before passing-out behind the wheel.

When I came-to, I was staring at a crew of burly construction workers leaning against their truck gazing at the sight of me. One of them said, "This guy is fucked up."

I was out for a good hour. Even though my clothes were drenched in sweat, I felt better. At least the fever was not as bad. I knew it would come back with a vengeance if I didn't get treatment soon. I bought some bottled water from inside the store, then checked Google for the nearest emergency clinic. I headed west on I-80 for the state line town of Windover.

I found the Community Health Center in West Windover, Nevada. They checked me in, then took my vitals and blood. Within fifteen minutes I was in an ambulance for the one hundred twenty-three-mile ride back to Salt Lake City. When I arrived at the Utah State University Hospital Emergency Room, a medical team was waiting.

They asked if I was Kenneth Sanford. I said, "Yes I am," and they took more blood. They put me in an isolation room to wait for the test results. The room was on the fourth floor; a nice room with a large picture window overlooking a courtyard with trees and a view of the city.

Forty-five minutes later the Infectious Disease Physician walked through the door. He trailed a nursing team who started an I.V. and hooked me up to a multi-monitoring vitals array. They were done before I realized it. I was connected to the mother-ship and was there to stay.

I didn't say a word. I wanted the doctor to speak first. He said hello and introduced himself. (This is where I admit, I don't have his name because I'm on lockdown orders from Governor Gavin Newsom. I'm in Campbell, California separated from my files. It's the Covid-19 Pandemic.)

He said, "Well, you have the Mersa." (MRSA Super bug, Methivcillin-resistant Staphylococcus aureus.) "You're going to be with us for a few days. Is that alright?"

I said, "It's a nice room and the view is great. I would be honored."

He smiled and replied, "I'll tell you; the MRSA is nothing to fool with. Something like this, you feel symptoms in the early morning and that evening, if you don't get the right treatment, you could be dead."

I said, "I know. I've had this before in California. They don't identify the strain of bacteria there. Four or five years ago this happened. They gave me a general antibacterial, then put me in an isolation room for ten days at fifteen thousand dollars a day."

He said, "You're lucky. This floor is new. I set it up primarily to care for infectious patients. We will take good care of you. And you won't be here for ten days. Five days at the most. I'll give you something to help you relax. You'll sleep better."

I said, "I don't use drugs. I don't want anything to make me groggy or euphoric."

He said, "Don't worry, it will only help you relax so you can get a good night's rest. Your body needs it."

I said, "Fair enough, you're the doctor and you seem like someone who knows what he's doing."

We exchanged a few minutes of small talk. Then he said he would check back with me later. I settled in and went to sleep.

Around midnight, I woke. I rolled over and placed my hand on the mattress. I felt different. I felt a surprising surge of strength. But there was something else. There was something helping me; something deep in every cell of my body. It was not human. 'This is beastly," I thought. That description proved more accurate later that day. I've never had this type of experience before, at least not that I could remember.

I'm a strong man, but strength is relative to how one uses it against a superior foe. My sister says, I look like a buffed senior. I don't know about that. The thing is, I knew this extraordinary entity was stronger than me and it was there to help.

I felt I needed to get into the right state of mind to honor this visitation. Plus I didn't want to mess up the chance at interacting with a wild-ass super power. How could I explain screwing-up something like this back at the Wednesday night poker game, for heaven's sake?!

At that moment, I reached up to get more comfortable. It was an effort, as if I was out of my element. I wasn't strained physically. I was making the effort so as to command the mattress to bend to my will.

I growled. I was startled at the deep resonance in my voice. I wasn't sure why I growled at the mattress as if it were a living thing to order about. Something in my mind wanted to take control of my welfare and it was showing me it was capable of doing just that.

I lay still wondering if this entity would violate my will or temporarily give me help, then leave me with a pissed-off Super-bug that wanted to kill me.

And what's with this Super-bug anyway? What are these killers doing making life more difficult than it already is? If these mindless germs want war, then war is what they will get, and so will their maker.

The idea that something wanted to kill every lifeforms on this planet cast a new light on the argument for staying healthy and tough as nails.

For the next three days, I growled like a bear. I growled like a gorilla, then like a dragon seeking whom he may devour. At times, I was intent on killing anything or anybody who came too close. Funny thing, at those times the hospital staff would walk by door but they would not come in the room. I heard their voices talking outside in the corridor, then I heard them keep on walking.

At regular intervals the staff would come in and do their routine maintenance. They would check my vitals and ask me what I would like to order for my next meal. I would answer politely and that was it. I didn't want anything else from them. I wanted to get back to making myself a weapon against this bacteria and everything else. I was on a power quest, and I knew what I was doing with the help of this entity.

In the morning of the third day the doctor came in and said my vitals looked good and I would be released by noon that day. I was out of danger. They would give me a bus ticket back to Windover, Nevada and I could be on my way. He said, "Don't worry. The bug is managed. I will give you a prescription for your out-patient treatment. You will not have any more recurrences from the MRSA."

I said, "Quite an experience, that treatment."

He said, "You did well. Now I have another patient waiting for this room."

I thanked him and said, "Keep up the work you do here."

"I will try," he said. "As long as I can, I plan to be here."

I thanked him again and said goodbye. He turned and went to look in on the other patients.

One of the nurses stayed with me to help me put my things in plastic bags and get my prescription filled downstairs. I was pushed out the front door in a wheelchair to wait for the Lyft driver.

Before I left, they handed me an envelope with a bus ticket and complimentary tokens for the craps tables at several casinos in Windover, Nevada. I also got a ticket for the free buffet at the Montego Bay Casino Resort. They have done this before.

The seafood buffet was to die for. Which I almost did but what a treat.

ABOUT THE AUTHOR

Kenneth R. Sanford is an American author and speaker. Formerly, Chief Scientist for a Silicon Valley based firm, he has completed two tours at Stanford Linear Accelerator Center. He has finalized eight years of independent research in the Astrophysics Physics Department at Stanford University, School of Humanities. He served as a military contractor for the United States Department of Defense and the Department of Energy for over seventeen years. He resides in the San Francisco Bay Area where he has lived for more than fifty years.

**LEGION'S RIDDLE TRILOGY
5 Star Review**
by: Jack La Rocca, PhD
Jan 20 2019

Brilliant. . . A celebration of human ingenuity: (and) the purest example of Real Sci-fi in modern times. Utterly Compelling Reading.
The author offers believable sci-fi based on a life of adventure.
Highly organized, allowing the reader to let go of guessing and just enjoy the adventure. Filled with intrigue and solutions to match each conquest.

**NEW BOX SET
NOVEMBER 2019**

LEGION'S RIDDLE TRILOGY
eBook

www.Legions-Riddle.com

NEW RELEASE
NOVEMBER 2019
PAPERBACK EDITION 6 X 9
LEGION'S RIDDLE TRILOGY

www.Legions-Riddle.com

RELEASE DATE
2020

BLACKHOLE

Alien soldiers get sentenced to death, or serve life in paradise on a world populated by the enemy. Throughout generations they stay and fight for survival.   Records of where they originate   become   lost.   Competition   over planetary domination is futile. The two races, at last, join forces to save their dying planet. On a mission, they set course to harvest light particles for warp-drive. Their destination, the feeding frenzy at the center of a BLACKHOLE.

"Extraterrestrial contact is inevitable," said Kyle, leader of the rogue civilization

"And so is the end of creation," retorted the Emperor Legion. "Primordial elements expel in the moment of the big bang. Light particles jettison to a cosmic soup. From there the leap to spacetime began. The light particles expand from the smooth tidal waves of dark energy. Perpetual forces brought forth galaxies, star systems and planets. Now, we set the cosmic bridge as we did at Temple Starbase."

RELEASED FEBRUARY 2020

HEALTH, WEALTH & HAPPINESS
THROUGH THE POWER OF THE SENSES

www.Legions-Riddle.com

Made in the USA
Las Vegas, NV
10 October 2023

78894259R00080